FOR JO

First published in the United States by
Ideals Publishing Corporation
Nashville, Tennessee 37214

First published in Great Britain by
Walker Books, Ltd.
London, England

Text and illustrations © 1990 by Chris Riddell

Riddell, Chris.
The wish factory/Chris Riddell.
p. cm.
"First published in Great Britain by Walker Books, Ltd.,
England"--T.p. verso.
Summary: Bothered by a nightmare about a monster, Oliver is taken
by a cloud to the Wish Factory
to receive the wish of his choice.
ISBN 0-8249-8482-X
[1. Nightmare--Fiction. 2. Dreams--Fiction. 3. Wishes--fiction.]
I. Title
PZ7.R41618Wi   1990   90–34473
[E]--dc20   CIP
                                         AC

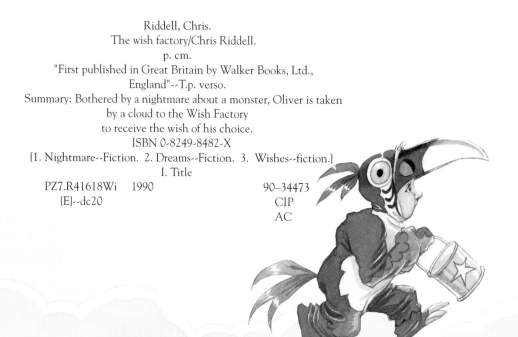

Printed in Hong Kong by South China Printing Co. (1988) Ltd.

THE
WISH FACTORY
Chris Riddell

Ideals Children's Books • Nashville, Tennessee

Oliver used to have
a bad dream about a monster.
But one night a cloud came
instead of the dream...

and carried Oliver into
the big, blue night...

far, far away to the Wish Factory.

Oliver closed his eyes and thought a big wish.

Then the wish-makers made
it good and strong…

and wrapped it up to keep it fresh.

"We hope it comes true," they said.

Then Oliver was in his own bed
and dreaming…

THE BIG BAD DREAM.

and the wish came true.

The monster wasn't big anymore, and it wasn't bad. "Boo!" said Oliver.

And morning came quite soon.